THE ALLURING TALES

Rupsa Das & Mohan Kabra

FanatiXx Publication

AM/56, Basanti Colony, Rourkela 769012, Odisha
ISO 9001:2015 CERTIFIED
Website: *www.fanatixx.in*

"THE ALLURING TALES"

By: Rupsa Das & Mohan Kabra

ISBN: 978-93-89557-76-3

English Poetry & Quotes

1st Edition

BOOK FORMATTING: MAYURI VALANJU
BOOK COVER: SAGAR SAMAL
PRESENTED BY: REASONS AND LAUGHTER

DISCLAIMER

This is a work of fiction. Our editors have tried their best to edit the content of all the author/authors and check the plagiarism. All the write-ups in this book are unique and are only published in this book.

In case any plagiarism or error is found, the author is the sole responsible and not the publisher.

ACKNOWLEDGEMENT

The Alluring Tales is an anthology which keeps so many emotions within its pages.

Thanks to everyone on the Reasons and Laughters to make this book get published. Special thanks to Japneet Kaur who cooperated and helped us so much in this work and helped in every possible way. She clarified the doubts at 1 A.M. at night for us.

Thanks to the Compilers, Rupsa Das and Mohan Kabra who had given their best efforts to make this reach at a height and make this book successful. No matter what, we had completed it in spite of many complexities. The best thing was we never gave up and hold on to each other and make this happen.

Thanks to our editor, Davesh Jain who played the role of an editor, promoter as well as a writer too. From reading early drafts to forcing us to complete it on time to edit it perfectly to giving great ideas which make our work easier.

Thanks to all the writers who trusted on us and gave their writings to get it published. You were really patient and cooperative. Also, special thanks to those who referred it to many people.

Lastly, a special note to all the readers that this book has a compilation of various emotions which one either faced or have seen others experiencing and you. So, please refer this book with other people so that all our hard work gets counted and the writers too get appreciated.

COMPILER

RUPSA DAS

Rupsa Das, an 18 year old, English literature student, born in Siliguri and studying in Kolkata. She is a passionate writer and pen downs her emotions through words.

She is a co-author of two anthologies and loves to dance, read books, explore new places and meet new people. She also has an experience in open mics and loves to spend time in social communities. She turns her goals into dreams. Dreaming to be an editor, she's working hard on it.

Here comes our compiler and writer who have given her best to make this anthology successful and touch the heart of the readers.

Instagram : @rupsaaaa._ .

Co - Compiler

MOHAN KABRA

Mohan Kabra, hailing from Siliguri, is currently pursuing B.Sc. He keeps keen interest in taking part in writing competitions and inking down his thoughts and emotions adding beautiful rhymes in it. He has been a co-author in an anthology and plans to write in more. He aspires to become a successful businessman.

Also, he's working really hard for his Instagram pages : @Wordfeeders @chand_lavzon_ki_kahani

Instagram : @devilz_god

FOUNDER

JAPNEET KAUR

Japneet Kaur, daughter of Mr. Surjeet Singh and Mrs. Dilpreet Kaur was brought up in Indirapuram, UP. She is pursuing German language and BA programming course from Delhi University. She is a passionate writer who loves to pen down her emotions and environment and strive to make her parents proud. She is even working on her very first novel making her one step closer to her goal.

Instgram : @sheedreamss

EDITOR

DAVESH JAIN

Davesh Jain, a 20 year undergraduate student from Gangtok, East Sikkim pursuing Bachelors in Travel and Tourism Administration. Loves to travel and blog and capture every moment through clicks and papers which captivates the heart. He writes to rhyme and sync which goes on in his mind and allures the people with his overwhelming words. Being a Basketball player and a Mixed Martial Artist brings him the urge to win every challenges which is set. Here comes our writer, editor and promoter who has given his best and cooperated in this anthology to its fullest.

EDITOR

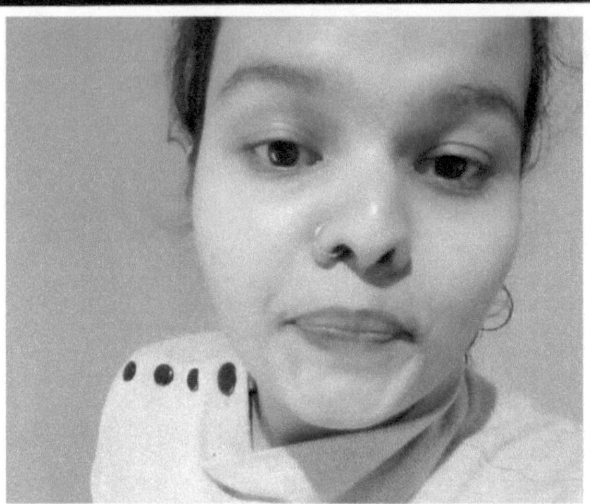

MAYURI VALANJU

Mayuri Valanju, resident of Mumbai. She is a commerce graduate pursuing higher education. Social Media Head of Fanatixx and Fanatixx Publications. Co-author of many anthologies. Her debut book is 'Spectrum of Thoughts'. Writing is Peace for her. She is addict of Korean, Turkish and Chinese dramas. Coffee is her love and sound of book pages flipping like her the most. Connecting with people and talking to them is what she loves.

You can find her on instagram @scribblers_abode.

DESIGNER

SAGAR SAMAL

Sagar Samal is a Photographer, Image Manipulation and Colour Grading Artist.

Hardworking with a "Create Something Awesome" Mentality.

A graduate in Bachelor of Computer Application but an Artist By Heart.

Instagram : photosign.cf

QUOTES

<u>Shounak Das</u>

- Falling into love with a person cannot be seen as an ultimate nirvana.

- It's not who you want to spend your Friday night with. It's who you want to spend your all day Saturday with.

- No one cares if the bottle is half empty or half full. Now all they care about is whether the glass is trendy and whether it would make them look cool.

- You can't people you love to tell you how you should love.

<u>Neha Agarwal</u>

- For cupids behold our love,
  No one can separate us.

- Emotions want to speak but heart doesn't let
  them out.

- Darling, you are strong enough to have a restart.

- Brave wings fly the highest.

<u>Shubha Brata Saha</u>

- You are the poem I came up with when I was searching for words.

  - Don't make a rush,

    Near your crush,

    To say that you do blush,

    Whenever she hush.

- Love is when all the imperfections cannot, after your feeling of perfection for them.

- The hardest thing in the world is to make a shattered heart believe and fall in love all over again.

Ishika Verma

- The way tears fall every night amaze me as they are constrained by unconditional pain and never ending thoughts.

- Don't blame people for smoking cause there's some,

  Who smokes down to filter to get lost in their emptiness,

  They smoke till they get choked to death.

- My Life is a Lie, my tears are now dry.

  I don't show but most of the times I cry.

  I want to give up all confinement and want to fly very deep above the sky.

  Sometimes I really wish to die

  But don't want to say my loved ones bye.

- I know I'm a liability,

I know I don't have an ability.

I don't care about anyone's nobility.

Yes, I'm not the one who could be anyone's viability.

I'm a liability and

I'm perfectly okay with this reality.

I know I'm a liability,

Kavya Khanna

- I feel like a burnt paper whose ashes still have your essence.

- Unable to breathe,

Struggling for sight,

Stuck in the cage of atrocities inflicted upon her.

She has lost herself to all the nights.

- The existence somehow lost its meaning,

There is no definite cause.

For now what I find is myself is nothing,

But a bucket full of flaws.

- She walked past the snow crowned mountains, admiring the glory of the perfect land. It was like everything her eyes laid on was astounding scene with its distinct finesse. The sea carved itself as a kaleidoscope of a complete unvented world hidden deep in the breathtaking blue colossal, just like a chapter waiting to be told and about to unfold.

<u>Arijit Deb</u>

- She said I light up her darkness

So I considered myself as her Sun.

But alas did I know

That I was only the firefly

That glows in her darkest hours

And dies the moment the sun comes out.

- You left your heart at my doorsteps

But never intended to knock.

- My thoughts are like water,

My soul is like a boat.

I shall float in this

Visage of conception

And in this same notion

I shall drown too.

- My scars aren't potholes
  That you will fix.

  They are entire oceans,

  You'll drown into.

Jeffrey Rujen

- Optimists always find motivation to succeed,

But realists look for all possible outcomes and achieve
something right.

- People in love are like two poles of a bar magnet.

Once broken, they can never become like before,

As there are conflicting forces of attraction and repulsion.

Never let it break nor expect things to be as they were.

- You maybe the king of the whole universe,

Own everything your eyes see,

Command anything to do something,

But if you don't have love, you are nothing.

- Love isn't just a feeling,

It's more than physical healing.

<u>Danica Rayen</u>

- Love comes where there is care,

Care stays where there is a loyal heart.

- Similarity in something can't change the differences over everything.

- Present

"An attempt of making a best future past."

- Remember one thing, strongest bond may also have a weakest bend;

And weakest bend may also bind instead of blend.

Barkha Pandey

- I decorated my feelings on a piece of paper

  And placed it next to a red rose.

  It flew with the force of love in the air,

  I assume he will it someday, somewhere.

- Don't be ashamed of the scars.

  They make you who you are.

- I've stopped writing about my pain and agonies,
  my fears and sorrows.

  I only write about a happy girl and the love she borrows.

- If we only consider facts, there would be no place
  for possibilities.

Deepali Gond

- I was so bad in games that even after winning your love,

I lost you in my fate.

- Sometimes I just wonder what you did.

Just converted a heart filled with love, hope and spirit into a barren one.

Now, no flower blooms.

- I wish I could learn the art of knowing you.

- Hating you is a long way journey,

I couldn't even learn to unlove you.

RHYMING

POEMS

Mohan Kabra

Shadows and Thoughts

The shadows and thoughts are almost the same;
It varies for everything and the way they frame.

They are sometimes narrow and sometimes so wide,

People to people and the heart they have inside.

Some are awful and some are really superior,

It all depends on the way they are interior.

It changes every time depending on the source,

It's all about the way you observe and endorse.

Thoughts and shadows are always with us,

It never changes even if you crush;

It may chance, depending upon the time,

It will again appear with a new sunshine.

Rupsa Das

Oh boy, you've cast a spell on me,

Making me fall for you every day.

My heart is always yours and always will be

And I promise you to love in every possible way.

I feel myself strongly in my arm

And your warm fingers gently stroking my hair.

Baby, I'm completely allured by your charm

And come closer leaving between us no air.

I found you on the whim of fate,

While thinking that my eyes got stuck on you.

My heart said, "Come on, don't be late ",

To tell the words I've kept for you.

Davesh Jain

Suicide of a boy

"This is for the best", one sad cold night a boy sat in
his chair;
Picked up a gun as he ran his fingers through his hair.

He sat and cried as he thought everything that's
happened,

"Has all been my fault?", he said if I was gone,

This would all be better and he told her,

"I love you now more than ever";

He said "Trust me this is for the best, you will see

Cause after I'm gone no more fighting, you'll be free".

He grabbed a bullet and put it in the gun said,

"I love you so much but now I have to run", he said.

"I'm sorry, I can't take this no more.

I've let down so many people I wish I could go back to
before."

He hung up the phone and pulled the trigger,

looked down at his chest as the pain grew bigger.

His eyes filled with tears they started to pour,

As soon as his family ran in, he fell to the floor.

****

Shambhabi Gupta

Things have changed and people are gone,

Life is not going to be long.

The end has come and it is all over,

My life is not that simple and sober.

The illusion has broken and the truth is out,

I understood it wasn't love I thought about.

A relation carries the love of two,

But I realized only I was there and not you.

My love for you was not a lie,

I will always love you till I die.

****

Amlan Dutta

Numb Mind

As those hallucinations inside my mind ran wild,

I looked for my freedom but you are still in my mind.

Deceiving this reality, my thoughts began to rhyme,

How can I free myself from this numbness of time?

Escaping from this silence of my heart,

It wouldn't be possible without the aid of my own.

Just when I thought everything was perfect,

My life turned upside down and became a rolling stone.

Wasn't that simple, over the course of time?

In a touch of reality, I lost my mind.

I couldn't stop myself from falling over and over again,

I wanted to be free and leave everything far behind.

The mind then understood the urge of pain,

And decided to never, never look back again.

My heart still sings for the song of the sea,

Taking over my feelings and beats me.

Anisha Mehra

I write because of my satisfaction,

Not to impress or gain attention.

Say whatever you want to say,

But I write because I cannot say.

So hey, let me tell you a case.

Where my thoughts were all in a race

And my feelings forgot to tie its lace.

And then I fell for someone

Who made me feel insane.

And, you know what happened next,
My heart got a place to rest.

I gave him my hand to hold,

But all got arrested by the words he told.

I realized then,

My laces were still open.

This lace was just like an open case which I didn't know
how to face.

My mouth couldn't say what to do,

So my arrested hand got rested with a pen

And of the thought of the poem you just read.

****

Arghadeep Ghosh

Tears led my eyelashes down,

Till you took off my crown.

Suddenly you led me away from your heart,

When I was on my track,

To bring love for you on my cart.

You led my mouth zipped,

And in my mind, all the memories creep.

Your love will never come back to me,

But trust me, my love was really very deep.

Did you feel to knock the door?

Forcefully I was pushed down the shore.

The bloody waves pulled me back again,

But I couldn't resist myself to get away from my heart's pain.

<u>Nalini Ramnarayan Shukla</u>

The sun and stars,

All the trees and flowers;

All animals green and grey

And the Gods to whom I pray.

Also the milk and curd,

The bright windows and the dark pits.

They all form my world,

Seep into me bit by bit.

My eyes fall short of vision,

My tongue fails the sense-talk mission.

My thoughts keep running in the world

And aimless zeal they wish to conquer.

All my being is just a comprehension of this world;

Who knows may be, in reality,

It is something even more absurd.

Bit by bit,

The world seeps into me

And bit by bit,

I sink into the world.

****

Surjamit Bhattacharjee

INVITATION

Will you go with me,

Where love is free?

Free from dirty dust of lust,

Free from all fragile trust.

Free from Petty yours and mine,

Free from what is non divine,

Will you sing along,

The lovely song?

A song about two hearts turn one,

A song about how love has won.

A song that melts you inside out,

A song that you can't stay without.

Will you go and dance

And feel the trance?

A dance that paints the soul with bliss,

A dance of love,

A dance of kiss.

A dance that makes our hearts go free,

A dance that cures all misery.

Let's do this hand in hand my friend

Until our time comes to an end.

****

Debashree Mali

Love Can Happen Twice

My heart was left alone

Until you came to make it your own.

You made me smile again

And I found myself healing from that pain.

Talking to you brings life to my soul,

And watching you smile brings happiness into my
bowl.

You've lit the spark of my life

And that's why I made my decision to make you my
wife.

Maybe we are different in opinions

But I will always respect your decision.

With the consent of our parents,

Let's be ready to write our new chapters

And make the famous quote true,

"Happily Ever After".

You were a coincidence in my life

But you made me believe that;

"Love Can Happen Twice"

****

Adrija Saha

The Wink of Karma

With ambitions that were ill hearted,

He was deceived by his own fate;

The King was outsmarted,

A pawn whispered, "Checkmate".

Broken and defeated,

The sinner accepted his downfall;

Karma gave a pat on his back,

The winner takes it all.

****

Nidhi Jain

Changes

People are changing around me,

They were the ones who cared about me.

Their priorities are changing

And they said that I am changing.

Their betrayal is as harsh as thunder,

Once they were my life no wonder.

Those changing faces depict my color blindness,

I showed them all my kindness.

They were the ones who controlled my anger,

And now, they are the reason of my anger.

It's all the game of importance which leads to changes;

Life will always come across changes,

But never lose any hopes and chances;

You'll be the same

And don't let people take your advantages.

Disita Sikdar

STILL

When the soul is fashionably sick,

The heart still chose wild thoughts to pick.

The mind says the thoughts are unsound,

Heart still searches for the fossil which is to be found.

The mind snatches the body to catch the light beam,

Poor heart still is busy seizing the dark old memories of
him.

My mind swallowing my pride,

Asked me to forget about that night.

Heart still grabbed those mindless dreams,

That oozes out like gleaming steam.

Mind says the heart is not a thing to play,

Heart still asks the nightmares to stay.

The mind asks the vanquish dreams to leave,

The heart still continues to weave.

Ticha Sonowal

Sour truth

Life is tough,

People are rough.

Fake and real is hard to identify,

But one day each of us has to testify.

The truth will get unravel,

No matter how far the lie would travel.

Falsity will get scattered like gravel,

While honesty will win the battle.

****

Ruchika Garg

Waking up at six,

The time is sharp fixed.

A quick cleaning of kitchen;

Tea, coffee and types of milk on mission.

She runs to room in as an alarming bell,

"C'mon, wake up, you're late as hell".

Next is the treasure hunt from the sea of our mess,

A lab copy, a file, a tie and lost parts of our dress.

Breakfast, all served, magically on the table with that extra bite,

She bids us all farewell.

Next moment she is in the house of prayer with all her devotion,

Praying for her family's health, safety and promotion.

Then comes the hectic work of cleaning up the home,

Each cloth soaked in foam.

Each dish scrubbed till shone,

Each furniture dusted like a throne,

Each corners mopped till stains all gone.

Finally, when she sits down with her meal,

Her naughty little ones will be arriving from their field.

In no time the bags will be thrown,

The shoes will be kicked, the wrestling will be on,

The ties will be whipped.

That "one" T-shirt will be searched, cupboard will be stripped,

The home will be a mess and continues the loop of same script.

****

Khushi Tiwari

Again

I never thought I would fall in love again,

But I did.

I never thought I would trust someone with all of me again,

But I did.

You have your flaws,

Maybe lots of those,

But you ought to have them 'cause baby you're a rose.

You make my days better,

You give me a smile, your flaws don't matter.

You make every moment spent with you worth a while.

Maybe I deserve better, maybe I really do.

But what do I do of all the love, I only got for you.

I like calling you mine,

I don't mind when you whine.

You aren't a need, a want you'll always be I promise to stay,

And listen to all you have to say,

I promise to love you through your good and bad days.

****

Bhaskar Malakar

Then again swallowed flame,

Set the soul free of blame.

Enchanted names at opposite of the one with a sword of
bloody blade.

We were to claim, tied hands in skin ripping chain,

Had to stand still till the end of this merciless game, kept
clashing in Sun, Storm and Rain,

Bare blood and ruthless in vein.

Injured yet pushed to the last lane.

No way out, no way in,

Nothing except suffering and pain.

Pumped out adrenaline, rushed out towards drain,

Fractured joints, displaced bones but high in brain,

Unleashed animals around, after all it was about to
entertain,

A street fighter of life I am at any stake, life was hardest and
so was I, say Amen.

FREE VERSE

POEMS

Japneet Kaur

And as dawn came down,
She laid herself in a coffin,
Far from everyone,
Poetry took birth the following day,
Her ripped heart that day stopped beating,
Her mesmerising soul evaporated somewhere in the sky,
People were mourning,
Tears weren't dried up,
That very moment her last poetry came to people's notice as they
looked up on the pink wall beside her photographer ready to be
honoured by garland full of poetries sang by the flowers in it,
And her last poetry said: As my body is set to be buried, please
don't cry,
Because a writer never dies,
Feel me in the wind, the rain which will shower in the name of
love, sound so poetic with words unheard and that is the beauty
of the nature which will cry out loud for me to get a life,
But I promise I will never die,
I m alive in the poetries unsaid,
The verses unheard,
As the rain pours down,
Remember, that is me,
Performing my other piece of poetry,
At that very moment, look above with a smile,
And praise my work,
It won't take much time.

****

Swapnasree Saha

The successful orphan girl had been waiting for that
night,

Where she could see the tiny moon with the love of her
life.

The stars will surround them to rejoice their
celebration.

The heavenly sky will bless them;

The night to witness their heavenly reunion.

All throughout the year she had been waiting for this
day,

How beautifully the sky met her celebrating Eid with a
smile!

****

Shweta Mazoomdar

The Birthday

It was her mother's birthday,

I recalled one fine morning.

My ten year old was excited,

Dancing merrily everywhere.

I arranged the blown balloons,

At the round corner of the house.

Taking a red paper she drew her,

"I made mom", she said innocently.

She placed a tiny cupcake,

I lit candles on it.

Seeing the tiny efforts I wondered,

How lucky is her mother to have her!

At twelve she woke me up,

Held my hand and took me to her.

There we stood holding our hands,

"Happy Birthday", we wished to the picture adorned with flowers.

Apoorva Singh

Odd One Out

Socially banned, legally approved;

Me as girl, stand in spot light.

Some says morning, some says dusk;

Brown beauty, needs the foundation touch.

Puny steps, timid voice;

One with long hair, is a perfect bride.

"I allow you to work and enjoy your life ", said husband.

The sentence shows that a man is having forward thinking

And is in favor of women empowerment.

No, read the sentence again.

The sentence itself shows his authority.

Freedom is not given,

It is born with you.

Just feel it and achieve it.

This thought was read twice;

In my writing skills,

It was "ODD ONE OUT ".

****

Sanjiban Bhowmik

Tik tok,

Time stop.

The closed room.

The empty brain,

The empty wallet.

The billion dollars,

The million fears.

The old past,

Which was vast.

The flower vase on the table,

The knife on the shelf.

The life in a thorn,

The rose is dead.

Bipasha Dey

I saw, I smiled and I blushed.

The brightness on that face made me smile

And I fell in love.

Never ever I imagined something

So soothing, so admirable,

So radiant, so attractive

And it was just more than perfect for me.

The moment I stared at;

There was a feeling of placidness,

Stillness within myself.

With no eager anticipation,

I felt in my chest a slow calm

Unfamiliar beating that exactly felt

Like a love song from 90's

Started being so beautiful

And a beautiful song started buzzing

In my ears in silence.

And the love,

I felt within myself then made me realize

That I will never fall out of love.

And staring at that particular thing endlessly

Made me fall in love again and again.

But, as the dark lanes were growing more insecure,

There was no better place than home.

For me, being a moon lover is really tough

Because I cannot stare at the thing I love the whole
night.

****

Debarati Mallick

How about losing myself into the woods

And never finding back the path that leads me into this
floor of green cover?

How about discovering a new way which would lead me

To a complete different city with different culture?

How about learning their story?

How about running into the peak

And freeze myself in the ice?

How about running into the falls

And play with the falling giant?

How about falling down

And bruising myself?

How about chasing after the bird

And lose my way in search of its home?

How about falling in love

And come up with a broken heart?

How about abandoning you only

To find my way back into the shelter of your arms?

How about feeling life draining away

With every passing day?

How about breaking the false sense of security

And feed the soul with taste of freedom?

How about leaving behind footprints on a beach just

To be washed away by the waves?

How about closing my eyes to an eternal sleep?

****

Sunrit Dutta

Deep down the alley,

Your subtle expressions hide.

Your presence brings forth,

Peace brings forth the reason to live.

Deep down the alley,

Where truth strives to reborn;

Deep down the alley,

Where thoughts prevail.

In that darkest corner,

I see you brightened by the copper sun.

Fed by the cool breeze

And enlightened by my love.

Deep down the alley,

It all ends, you and me.

Our dreams fated here.

Santoshi Agarwal

PROMISE FROM A LONG DISTANCE LOVER

I can't promise you that the wind will not be cold in
future;

But I can promise you that I will always be the bonfire
whenever you need.

I can't promise you that I will stop the waves which
may shatter your dreams;

But I can promise you that I will always help you to
build your dream place near the shore.

I can't promise that I will wipe your tears and solve
your problems;

But I can promise that I will always be there with you
till the sun rises from the east.

I can't promise that there will be no dark clouds in our
romantic journey;

But I can promise that I will always be the rainbow to
fill colors in your life.

I promise you that I will not cry while thinking that
why are we so far away;

But I need a promise from you that you will never
make me realize the distance between us

And must be proud with what they have.

Now is the time for you to be stable in what you have.

****

Roshni Khamluwa Rai

Love included all the peace, care and understanding

Till I met you;

Drunk in all the wine that helped me sink

Even above the sky,

Slowly cursed myself falling

Into that stoned eyes.

Some sip of tears,

Some indulge with commitment;

Partially realizing how everything comes to end

Of my self independence,

Fractionally making me conscious

About the truth of being yours.

Some colorless and some odorless,

Some with ounce of selflessness and some carelessness.

I vigorously jumped into your open arms,

Looking into your empty lap,

I fall crazily asleep.

That thought of mine to keep you only with me

Haunts me every single day,

Kissing that every inch of glue

To get stuck in your heart.

****

Lehar Gupta

People will say scars are sign of weakness,

Trust me it is not;

Rather you have survived from so much of trauma.

I know these scars have stories which are unheard,

But they show how on Earth,

The pain you bore.

The scars on you which I have seen,

Often you tried to hide them so unclean.

Trust me, your scars say,

"The dark days will pass, hold on strong as the deepest
wounds at long last heal".

My poem says million little things to me

And I know your scars do the same.

My each poem covets to tell a story,

"What are your stories behind those scars?"

Everyone at a stage feels,

Life is tiring,

But look, still we all stand tall.

Therefore if any trauma occurs,

"Need not fall";

There are situations when we don't triumph over the fights,

But dear, look at it carefully,

You will see a loop hole which guides towards light.

****

Dipmol Bumzon

Some words failed to get voiced,

Some feelings failed to get expressed,

Some emotions hidden inside my diary.

I knew that love hurts

But never knew love can even make you a prisoner of your own thoughts.

I gave away everything I had.

Even my soul is part of yours now.

Only thing I got was those memories.

Living inside this prison of memories is so beautiful.

Sometimes it makes me cry, it makes me blush and sometimes it makes me go to past and pinch myself whether those were just a dream or an illusion.

I don't care even if it was just an illusion.

I would love to live in illusions where I can find you and me becoming 'us' because Reality is so painful

And there inside my head a voice whispers, "You can't build an empire just with memories", I realized, I felt.

I cried, tears were trembling down from my neck.

Yet, I am building this prison for myself.

Why? Have you ever questioned yourself?

Trust me! No one can give the best answer than yourself.

One thing I realized by living inside this prison of memories.

No one was ever taught this language, never need to learn it.

Regardless of what language we speak or what nationality we are;

We all speak one precious language of the world and that is 'Love'.

Yes. It is within you and me.

Love is innate and I understood sometimes we don't need to express it as our eyes are the window to soul.

I can see how much you love me and you know how much I love you.

Then why these sacrifices? Why this pain? Just why? I questioned myself again.

The voice whispered, "It is true that the other name of Love is Sacrifice."

I didn't lose you. I didn't lose my love.

In fact, my love won. It's a victory. I smiled.

It's true that I can't touch you, see you;

Even though you may never be by my side, yet I can always feel your presence.

You may not be here physically but I believe in spirituality and you exist immaterially.

Love always wins!

Love is always in the moment and I can feel you everywhere.

In those light of dawn to dusk, those stars and moon of midnight.

You are always inside my heart.

No matter the situation is dark or light.

****

<u>Oishi Banerjee</u>

The old gramophone on my desk was bought on a
whim

And it kept playing these unnecessary songs.

Love was a gramophone, I thought.

It played back unnecessary old memories.

The paint on my nails was not perfect

As they were chipped off at different corners

And the beauty was no more but I didn't remove the
rest.

Love was cheap nail paint, I thought.

Imperfect, got eroded quickly yet leaves back

Stuffs you want to hold on.

The dried flowers pressed inside my book were kept as
reminders of adventures I had

And they made me feel very brave 'cause I faced them.

Love was like those flowers, I thought.

It had made me feel brave.

The tea leaves in my tea on dull mornings diffuse with
the water that had no color

And instantly made it fragrant and vibrant.

Love was like tea leaves, I thought.

It added color to all the dull mornings or nights.

The rainbow I saw yesterday was so prominent and
colorful that it made me

Forget about the preceding storm that made me feel
broken.

Love was a rainbow, I thought.

It only appeared after the storm ended.

Todi Dutt Mazumder

Love is a sin

Every lover

Is a cold blooded murderer,

Just trying to escape from a sin,

She had committed

(Breaking a heart).

Love is unreciprocated

(Is it even Love if it is reciprocated?)

No one would tell you

That when you fall in love,

You'll feel you're in a world

Where every thing is beautiful.

But who would know,

Beauty is in hatred too.

Sayani Nath

STORY OF THE WAVES

The waves which wash the left out footprints on the shore.

Those were heavy with lots of memories.

The waves gather them to the depth of the sea,

The sea stores them with itself

To make us forget about them.

This sea contains so much emotions in its depth.

Though it looks beautiful!

Like it contains numerous lives with various tales with them.

That's kind of our lives, right?

Like in our lives, we face various moments with different kind of emotions.

But with the flow we move on, we keep them in our heart's depth.

And our lives go on and on!

That's wonderful to dream of,

To find stories in every corner of the nature.

To get lost in the far horizon!

****

Mayank Jain

Writing the unwanted

Dear Mom and Dad,

If you are reading it, I am dead.

And even if I tell you not to, you will cry.

It was difficult for me to write this letter but it will be harder for you to read this.

The pen was ponderous when I was writing what possibly could be my last words

And also, because I wished it would have never reached you

Instead, I would have been there to hug you.

Mom and Dad,

Please be proud of your deceased son who sacrificed himself for our home.

You must be angry, you must be sad and I am really sorry about that.

Tell my friends that they were the best,

tell my sister to forgive me for all our fights,

tell my brother to take my car he always wanted to have

and tell my lover that I am sorry for being late for our date.

I don't know if I would be going to heaven or hell

But I will always remember mom's Sunday's special,

Oh my mouth waters just by remembering its taste and smell.

Mom, please take your medicines on time

Dad, I will always regret not getting a chance to drink together

Damn! Writing this letter bringing your brave warrior to tears.

Mom and Dad,

I wished I could have said it forever

I love you more than you can love me together.

From Your Kid

who wants you to smile when remembering me

But if you will cry remembering me,

Then forget me forever.

****

Jayoti Mondal

My anxious self to me

Oh! How I wish I could've stopped those loud voices
calling out inside my head;

Filling me up with deep despair and loneliness.

No, its roots have gone deeper and now I can't get rid
of it.

I see people all around me, I try to speak but my voice, I
can't hear it.

I feel like a burden and I keep myself away. Build walls.

Oh! How happy would I be, if I stop being anxious all
the time.

I only pray that the voices deep inside me that they die
someday but they only keep getting stronger.

They pull me into the dark abyss. They blind me.

If only I could get rid of them. Wouldn't it be so nice to
have a peace of mind?

But they keep winning. And I lose.

Every day.

Zahabiya Nathani

Well it was that time, when winters were high and
summers were lured.

It was that place, crowded but everyone felt alienated
and life happened fast and livelihood became paced.

It was the month of love,

The year of millennium and the life of eternal,

The life that breathe with hopes high.

And they met for the first time when tides were high
and the sun set to die.

****

<u>Sanya Chugh</u>

Time flies,

People leave.

Leaves us with memories

And recalling them touches us

Just like the rain touches the roasting desert.

Just like the wave of cool breeze

Giving a relief in a hot burning day.

They make us laugh,

They make us cry.

Time flies

But memories never die.

****

Ishpreet Kaur Maskin

Someone I know, who I turn to,

Someone who I call for.

Someone who always brought beam on my face,

Someone who I cannot bare to mislay in any case.

Someone who always says that I am just a call away,

But still yearn her every day.

Someone who sometimes brawls with me,

But still has a special place in me.

Someone who all the time took my hand

And showed me the way through

And she calls herself my sister,

Whom I can turn to.

Akanksha Choudhary

Those unforgettable nights

When we had unsolved fights,

Those tight hugs in thousand bucks,

Those moments of jealous were really fabulous,

Those holding of hands,

I know that you understand

You are the untouched pure petal

That I would never let anyone pluck.

****

Disha Jaiswal

Wind blows and the flashback starts.

The first thing I see is my little doll

Which used to carry all around

And now it's pretty that no where it is found.

I remember the times when mom behind me

To finish the glass of milk that never used to drink.

Remember the time when a small chocolate with glitter my face

And I used to jump with happiness all the way,

I remember days when every small cut would tear me up,

But it seems funny that now physical wounds no more hurt;

The heart is heavy but the lips still smile.

I just wish that the life would be rewind.

Kinshuk Jain

Lost Friend

We all have a person saved in our contact list as favourite.

To whom we have shared our feelings and deepest secrets.

No matter how hard the life may seem,

Just by talking to them it all starts to feel right

And even if they are not available, their profile pictures are enough.

But today, that picture doesn't feel alright,

It failed to calm the noise of my emptiness,

It failed to provide me comfort,

It failed to bring me back the smile

Which I discovered because of her.

Chandrima Saha

From his early school days, people stained his identity with a characterless mark. For his father abandoned him and his mother after his birth. Not able to take responsibilities, his father escaped without giving a thought of the two innocent faces behind. Somehow, his mother consoled herself from the grief and started earning by doing random jobs to support their livelihood. Whenever, the son and his mother used to go out together, the society used to perceive his mother and comment on her character. His blood used to get ignited but listening to his mother's advice he somehow collected patience for the right time. Along with his studies, he started engaging himself in a part time job. But fate was really unfair with him, that he got the job of washing dishes in a neighbor's luxurious residence. But he hardly gave up on it and worked to save some money to buy a smart phone. Finally, the day arrived and he bought a smart phone with his years of savings because he has heard somewhere about the YouTube coaching videos for cracking government exams. By that time, he was a graduate and then managing an internet connection, he started watching YouTube videos for qualifying government exams. To manage the money for the form fill up and internet expenditure, he started selling newspapers and became a delivery boy. Meanwhile he was also looking after her old mother who has been observing her son to go through such tough battles. She motivated him and prayed to Almighty to direct the beacon of light in his budding life. After two years of rigorous hard work and dedication, he cracked the IBPS PO exam and success greeted him with flying colors. Now the same society, which used to comment on the character of his mother and looked the both with downgraded vision, now invites them in their houses and sings unstoppable praises for his son. The son of the proud mother now proved that character is not a label or a mark that is forcefully imposed on you. Character is built with one's actions, dedication, hard work and utmost faith.

****

Shaoni Mallick

TWENTY YEARS

A canvas- as empty as can be-

Stood alone in a corner.

Thirsty, it waited to get drenched in vibrant colors.

A few brushes were scattered on the ground,

The paints had dried away;

A long lost dripping sound.

Twenty years or so they say.

A sound of a rusty lock crack-open.

There she was-

A lady with a stick slowly moved across the room.

She sat down on the dust and sand

Her bare fingers drew a few strokes in the air

As she slowly picked up the empty canvas with her
hand.

Twenty years or so they say.

Memories flood in.

How mesmerized the people used to get by those hues!

Beguiled, they would stare at them for hours!

Oh! How she missed those days.

"Why did she give up?" You'd ask.

Retinoblastoma.

It was difficult for her when she lost her sight.

There wasn't a single night

When her canvas would not summon her.

But a fierce lady lived within,

Loss of sight wasn't a big thing-

The empty canvas got its wishes.

Twenty years until now.

Aadya Dang

That flower which you gave me has dried up,

That chocolate which you gave me has melted,

That love which you gave me has faded.

But surprisingly, that fake smile which you gave me,

Still confuses people

Because they know that with me,

You are no more there.

****

Co-Authors

I am Swapnasree Saha, a passionate writer and destined to mass communication.
Words of Caramel(a page for which I am working in) has described me as the "youngest of all musketeers, she has proven herself time and time again with her words".
I live in Siliguri also called "the gate of North Bengal".
I like to make hay while the sun shines, not only in writeups of different genre but also in abstract sketches.

I am Shweta. An intricately intricate nineteen year old who finds solace in reading books and exploring life in various unique ways. I've done my schooling from St. Joseph's High School Matigara and currently pursuing bachelor's degree in English.

Shambhabhi Gupta, 18years old
From Siliguri
College student
9614554398

Hola, I *am Aadya! I have just completed my schooling from Dehradun. I am from Delhi. An overthinker by choice and a writer by passion*

A Small Guy of 19,
in A Small Town Of Siliguri
Trying To Make Things Big,
In a World Owned By Giants.
(High School Science Seeker)
9474760864

I am Arghadeep Ghosh(Mr. Dot). I am from Siliguri, West Bengal. I am taking my education from D.A.V. school and is in 11th standard. You can contact me by phone or by WhatsApp - 8617691657. I also have a page on Instagram known as @mr.dot_official.369.

I'm sanjiban bhowmik of class 12 , a tigpian, I stay in Milan pally Siliguri and 8167509394 is my contact number

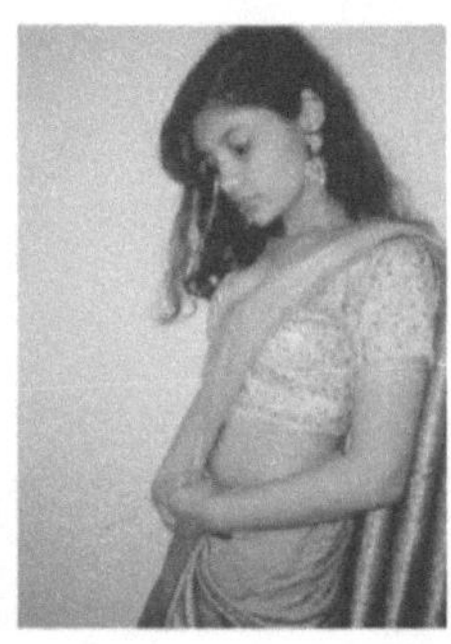

I'm ishika Verma
I'm from Bihar, My thoughts are a sad collection of 'maybes and almost'.

Bipasha Dey
Assam
Presently residing in siliguri
Doing better

My name is Debarati Mallick
I am from Siliguri
I am currently pursuing BDS from
Burdwan Dental college
Phone number 9800509527

Myself Sanya Chugh. I live in
Hanumangrah Rajasthan. I study in
11th standard. You can contact me on
9001930005 or 7888473637

Myself Sunrit and I currently pursuing BBA
LLB from Amity University Kolkata. I am
from Siliguri. Contact me @8637588549

Poems and you are the most beautiful art existing in the world.
Kavya Khanna
Delhi NCR
Completing 12th from Dehradun.
(Hostler)
9910967631

Amlan Dutta, a 26 years old free spirit who loves to explore the world at his own terms. He hails from West Bengal and currently living in Bangalore. A Layout Artist by profession, who has a passion for writing. He loves to read books, spending time experimenting with writing about life.

I am Akanksha Choudhary and I am from Delhi and I did my 12th from Dehradun. My phone number is 6204681820

Name- kinshuk jain
City- shamli(u.p)
Education- Bcom(hons) final yr
Contact no- 9058777742

Roshni Khamluwa Rai from Gorubathan,
persuing my bachelor degree in media science
from inspiria Knowledge Campus.
You can contact me via email
rairoshni691@gmail.com or WhatsApp and call
@ 9609557302

I am Nalini Shukla. I am an
engineer and an IT professional. I
like to scribble.

If you are a bit skeptic, trying to read between my thoughts.
Then just know I'm the cryptic, for I talk in coded words

Jeffrey Rujen, engineering student who has bloodlines of the 5 southern states and hails from the town of Hosur, studying in Delhi who's into music, writing, photography and dance.
IG: jeffrey_rujen_r
FB: Jeffrey Rujen

Ishpreet Kaur Maskin
From Ludhiana
An introvert at first but later a
Bubbly girl.

I *am lehar gupta. Studying in dehradun but lives in lucknow. I am pursuing medicine and interested in mass communication. I am an all india gold medalist in skating and a state level athlete.*

Dipmol Bumzon, lives in Siliguri west Bengal, studying media science in Inspiria knowledge campus.

She is Danica Rayen an Aeronautical Engineer & emerging writer from Tamil Nadu . She finds her own happiness in writing poems, quotes , stories and so on ..You can further follow her writings @vrayen8998 her insta ID.

I'm not a cigarette that you'll smoke and crush. I'm a drug baby you'll beg for me.

Zahabiya Nathani. Living in Mundra
A computer nerd with hearts for poems
Contact me: kish_mish53 on Insta

My name is Oishi Banerjee. I am from Kolkata. I am a undergraduate freshman.

My name is Debashree Mali
I am an English literature student
of 5th semester
And I'm from Tinsukia but
pursuing my graduation at
Dibrugarh.

Hey, I am Disha Jaiswal and I'am
from Siliguri, West Bengal. I'm in
my 1st year persuing B.sc economics
from Salesian College Siliguri
Contact no :- 9679706217
Insta I'd:- disha_jaiswal__

I am Adrija Saha, 18 years old. Residing
at a humble house in Kolkata with
family. I was a student of Mahadevi
Birla World Academy. Presently studying
English honours in Bidhannagar college.

I *am Barkha pandey, from siliguri,
studying at north point residential
school, standard* 10, *contact-*
7047931165, 7430061189

*My name is ShubhaBrata
Saha
I am From Siliguri.*

*Hi, My name is spelled and pronounced as
Bhaskar Malakar. I am from a small town
named as Kailashahar, Tripura,India.I
have been finishing my Civil Engineering
degree.Quite passionate about these artistic
activities like writing and all. Thank you.*

I'm Chandrima Saha. I'm from Guwahati, Assam. I have completed my graduation in science stream. My hobbies are framing my thoughts, singing, making videos and analyzing situations.

I *am Todi Dutt Mazumder, currently in class* 12. I *am from Kolkata.*
Contact details : 9874634952

I *am Sayani Nath,*
From Kolkata.
I'm *studying now in Standard* XI.
Phone Number :- 8335854033

This is Mayank. A little fatty who loves to eat, watch animes, binge Netflix and web series and enjoy superhero, science fiction, and fantasy movies. He got interested in poetry in class 5th and soon the world of novels and mangas and comic books intrigued him. Currently pursuing MBA from Manav Rachna International Institution of Research and Studies in Faridabad, a city which would soon stand tall with its neighbors. He is trying his earnest to complete writing atleast one book of his own.

Jayoti Mondal is a girl from Kolkata, pursuing B.Pharmacy from Jadavpur University.
She loves to write in her leisures and read books.
You can find her at facebook, her Instagram handle is joy_oh_tea.

Name - Deepali Gond
City - Indore
Education- Under Graduating Student
Contact - 7477208857, 8962194168

Ticha Sonowal
Tinsukia
Bsc in MBBT *at cotton university*
Guwahati
tichasonowalng@gmail.com contact no.
7002209636

Ruchika Agarwal
Siliguri
College student
ruchikagarg.9827@gmail.com

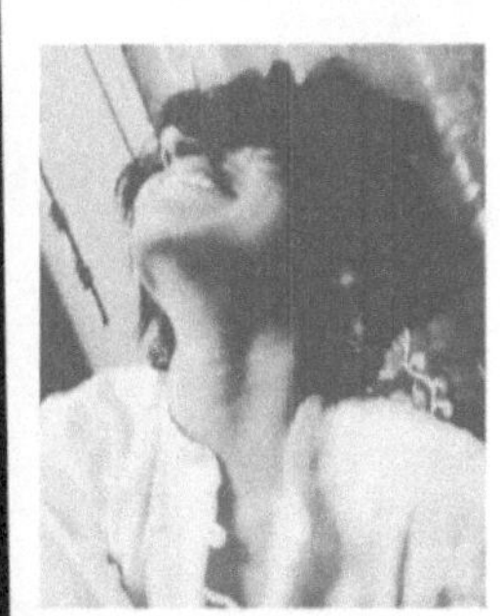

Hey! I'm Shaoni. I'm from Kolkata and I'm studying in Bethune College. Just trying to get found in this crowd. Catch me up on insta @titir_10.

I *am* Disita Sikdar. A small town girl with dreams in her eyes and miseries in life. I try to blot feelings in the paper to light up the stairs of mind and soul.

ABOUT REASONS AND LAUGHTER

Reasons and Laughter is a community which deals with providing services, compiling anthologies, organising competitions and Open Mics, found by Japneet Kaur.

Our main objective is to give a good platform to budding writers to help them grow, even to provide best services and giving wings to their dreams.

Email: ralservicess@gmail.com

Instagram: @reasons_and_laughter